A Tale of Shakespeare's Dog

CRAB & WILL

WRITTEN & ILLUSTRATED
BY
GREGORY MAGNUSON

Author's Note: Crab is the name of the dog in the play Two Gentlemen of Verona by William Shakespeare. Shakespeare was one of the greatest playwrights of all time and lived from 1564 to 1616.

Dedicated to Anna, Chloe and Wesley

ISBN 978-1-105-95102-2

Penned & Scribed by Gregory Magnuson

Act I

Words, words, words, Will Shakespeare loves to arrange them all day. Scribbling, sketching and rhyming, he enjoys the fun of writing a play.

Always by his side, his fond friend sits and listens. He is neither King nor Queen, Prince or Royal… It is his dog, Crab the loyal!

Crab's greatest wish is to have a speaking part in one of Will's plays.

The other day while Will was writing a script, he begged me to listen. "Crab" he said, "How about—To eat or not to eat?"

"Will!" barked I, "I was thinking 'to speak or not to speak?"

"Will", I howled "Please give me a line in one of your plays! Give me comedy, tragedy, history. I want a 'to be or not to be?' that is the question for a dog like me."

I inspire Will with some of his best lines. "The dog will have his day…" from Hamlet is poetry! And "When I open my lips, let no dog bark…" from Merchant of Venice chills me. It seems only fitting that he give me a part.

He made a silly face and went back to dipping his quill in the inkwell. I decided to take matters into my own paws…

So off I went to the Globe Theater in London— the perfect place to learn about acting, writing and plays. No time like show time to ask the other actors about the perfect line for Crab.

I bumped into Hamlet. We bury bones together in the round shadows of the Globe Theater. "So, Hamlet, you have some great lines. What do you see a good looking dog like me playing?"

Hamlet cleared his throat, "I see you as a princely monarch, Prince Crab of Denmark!"

"Brilliant!" I woofed.

I pranced into the costume room. King Crab sounded good to me, except there was one problem. The costumes were too big, I am only three feet tall.

Suddenly my stomach howled with hunger, I knew just who to see...

Falstaff always had plenty to eat. "How are you my friend?" he belched and tossed some treats my way.

"Do you have any ideas for parts I can play or a line I can say?" I asked with a mouth full of food. "How about playing Romeo's friend? You can tell Juliet that Romeo loves her."

No Way! That Romeo is crazy. The last time I saw him he tried to put me in a dress and then he smeared lipstick on my chops. Yuck!

Suddenly one of the costume dressers scooped
me up. He stuffed me in tights, put something
on my back and sprinkled me with pixie dust.
He shoved me on stage in front of hundreds of
people playing…

A fairy? On a midsummer night? This was a terrible sight. I'd rather be Romeo's girlfriend.

I was licking the fairy dust from my fur when Iago tried to lead me into a web of unkindness.

He whispered in my ear a part I did not
want. I slunk away and continued my hunt.

ill showed up. "Crab, my floppy-eared friend, I have the perfect part for you." He stuck a small scroll in my paw and rushed off.

Now?! I stepped onto the stage with Lance the clown. He recited: "I am the dog: no, the dog is himself, and the dog is me! What do you say Crab?"

I unfurled the scroll Will handed me, but the page was blank! Not a drop of ink stained the parchment. I had to take a risk and speak true. I cleared my throat and dramatically...

"Woof, woof, woof" I called with all my might.

The crowed cheered and laughed. I received a standing ovation from all those in the pit. The line was a hit. At that moment I realized the words belonged to all those that set foot (or paw) in the Globe. The part I played and the lines I said were up to me. Will said, "All the World's a Stage."

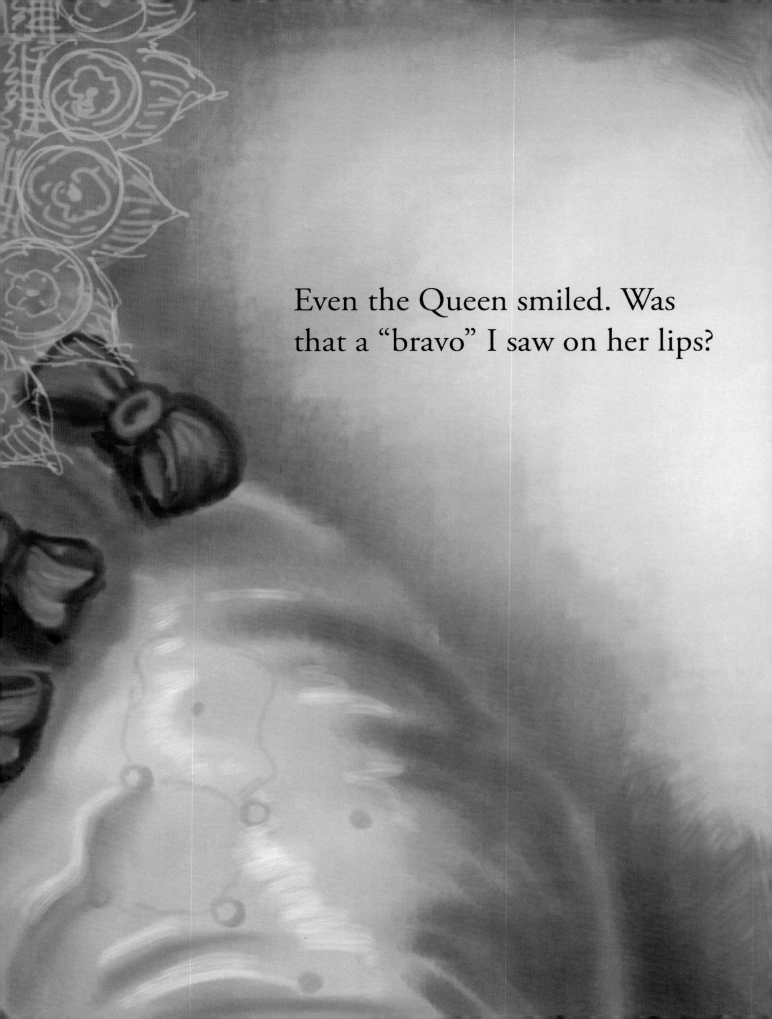

Even the Queen smiled. Was that a "bravo" I saw on her lips?

And that is how Crab found his very own role in one of Master Shakespeare's plays. It was a soliloquy appropriate for a dog of his pedigree. As the night follows the day, Crab found a line in his own play.

"All the world's a stage,
And the ~~men~~ dogs and ~~women~~ cats

merely players ...
And one ~~man~~ dog in his

time plays many parts ..."

-William Shakespeare

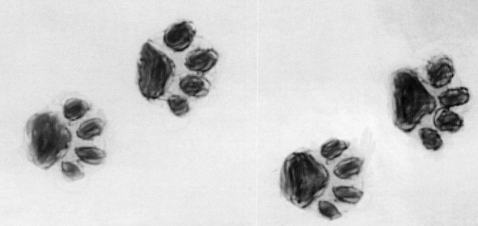